Mary Grae

Be Inspired!

MW00901557

To Lesley for falling in love with a six week old ball of lavender fur.
Thanks to Boomer for inspiring this story and
making me laugh every day.----PJP

To little sisters Audrey and Kaelan.----A. O. I.

Tree Of Life Publishing
Peeper & Friends
P.O.BOX 421004
Summerland Key, FL 33042
www.treeoflifepublishing.com
www.peeperandfriends.com

Copyright 2003 by Peter Parente.

All rights reserved, including the right of reproduction in whole
or in part in any form
without written permission from the publisher.

Published by Peeper & Friends
an imprint of Tree Of Life Publishing 2004.

Printed in Hong Kong.

Library of Congress Control Number: 2004096006

Parente, Peter
Boomer To The Rescue / by Peter Parente:
illustrated by Aleksey, Olga, Ivan Ivanov

ISBN 0-9745052-3-4

BOOMER
TO THE
RESCUE

STORY BY
PETER PARENTE

Illustrated by A&O Ivanov
Computer design Ivan Ivanov

Boomer and Roger were excited to make friends with all of the other forest creatures tomorrow at their first day of school.

Boomer said, "I'm kind of nervous."

Roger asked, "Why?"

"Maybe the others won't like me because I'm lavender," Boomer explained.

Momma Skunk overheard the boys talking and asked, "What's not to like?"

"I don't look like you and Papa," Boomer replied,
"or any other skunks."

"Being different is not bad.
It makes you who you are," Momma answered,
"No two creatures are exactly the same.
We all have different shapes, sizes, colors
and even smells. That's what makes us all special.
It's what is on the inside that matters."
"Do you mean inside, like our tummies?" Boomer asked.

"No, silly," Momma explained, "our hearts. Roger may be smaller than most animals in the forest, but he has a heart even bigger than a grizzly bear. When you are kind and caring, your heart can be more than ten times the size of your body. Now it's time for you to get some sleep for your big day."

"Boomer, wake up!" Roger squeaked,
"The sun is up. The birds are singing.
It's time to go to school."

They scurried through the forest to the grand oak tree. School was being held by Mr. Featherby, the eldest owl in the woods.

Squirrels, raccoons, rabbits and all the other forest creatures gathered around.
Boomer proudly announced, "Hi. This is Roger, and my name is Boomer."

"What is that smell?" sneered Frankie, the squirrel,
"Your name should be STINKBOY. Roger, you can play with us
if you want to get away from the skunk."
"His name is Boomer! He is my best friend. We are all
different on the outside and that makes us special," Roger
told the squirrel.
"Yeah, but he stinks. If you are his friend then you stink too."
Frankie laughed as Boomer ran away.

Roger followed his friend to their favorite spot by the creek. "Boomer, don't be upset. When they get to know you they'll realize that you are the best friend anyone could have. They'll feel bad for teasing you."

"I just wanted to introduce myself and make new friends. They were mean. Maybe Momma was wrong and I'm not special," Boomer said sadly.

Boomer jumped up and asked, "Do you hear screams? Something is wrong at the school."

They ran back towards the school as fast as they could.
There they saw all of the other children cornered by
a mean grizzly bear.

"All these choices for breakfast, but who to eat first?"
growled the grizzly. "Squirrel makes a great
appetizer."

Frankie yelled, "Put me down or I'll..."

"You'll what?" the bear interrupted. "You are too small to be making any demands to me. All of you are too small to do anything except be a snack!!"

Something clicked in Boomer's head. He realized why he had a different smell, "Yes. Yes I am.
You can call me STINKBOY. Now smell my wrath!"

Boomer turned around,
smacked down his front paws,
raised his tail and let his special
powers take control.
The bear seemed to go into shock.
He dropped Frankie
and he stood
motionless.

The bear made his choice. He ran off into the forest apologizing, promising never to bother another creature.

All the forest creatures burst into cheers,"Boomer, Boomer, Boomer!"
Frankie walked up to Boomer and said, "Thank you for saving me, especially after how I treated you. You are the most special of us all. I did not understand that being different is a good thing."
Boomer smiled. "That's OK. I'm glad we can get to know each other for who we are on the inside and be friends."

Save America's Forests

For millions of years, North America was covered with Ancient Forests that evolved in a dynamic interaction of sunshine, wind, rain, fire, and thousands of different species. The oldest trees lived more than a thousand years. In the past few centuries, most of the original forests have been logged. Fortunately, the U.S. has a vast network of 152 national forests that are one of our nation's greatest natural treasures, and contain most of our country's last remaining Ancient Forests. The national forests are filled with wonders of the plant and animal kingdom, like mammoth Redwood trees that grow taller than a football field, giant Pacific salamanders over a foot long, and mighty hunters like grizzly bears. Millions of Americans visit our national forests every year to enter the deep greenery and experience the wilderness as Native Americans did generations ago.

During the 20th century, millions of acres of the national forests were clearcut for timber. The ancient trees were taken away, destroying the homes of animals like skunks and spotted owls that had lived there for millennia. After a forest is clearcut, rain can wash away the treeless, unprotected soil so that the Ancient Forests cannot grow back. The animals are forced to find new burrows, branches, and treetops to call their home.

Shortly after the first Earth Day in 1970, Carl Ross saw that forests in his New York suburban town were being bulldozed for development. He joined with other citizens in a successful effort to protect a remaining tract of forest that is now the only large natural forest left in his community. In 1990, Carl began a new nationwide coalition of citizens, scientists, and environmental groups called Save America's Forests, and then created a bill in the U.S. Congress, the Act to Save America's Forests. This bill would protect the last Ancient and wild forests and prevent clearcutting on our national forests, and would restore natural forests to the large areas that have been clearcut. World famous scientists like Dr. Jane Goodall and Dr. E.O. Wilson have visited Congress and told them to pass this historic legislation into law. Now your help is needed. You can learn more about how to protect and rescue our wild forests and the animals that live in them by visiting our website and telling Congress to save America's forests!

4 Library Court, SE
Washington, DC 20003
202-544-9219

www.SaveAmericasForests.org